W9-DGB-460

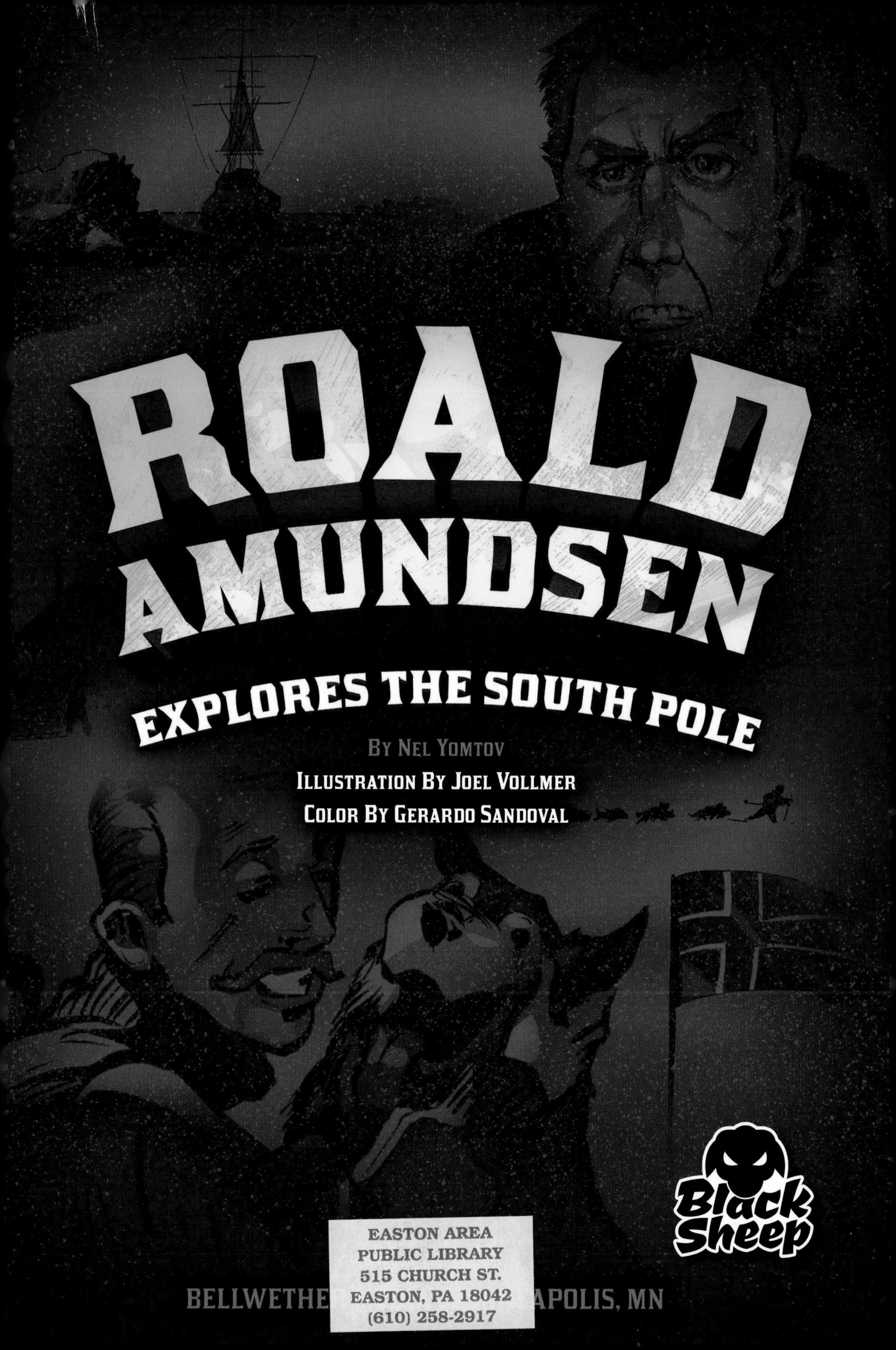

ROALD AMUNDSEN

EXPLORES THE SOUTH POLE

By Nel Yomtov

Illustration By Joel Vollmer

Color By Gerardo Sandoval

BELLWETHE … APOLIS, MN

Library of Congress Cataloging-in-Publication Data

Yomtov, Nelson.
  Roald Amundsen Explores the South Pole / by Nel Yomtov.
     pages cm. -- (Black Sheep: Extraordinary Explorers)
  Summary: "Exciting illustrations follow the events of Roald Amundsen exploring the South Pole. The combination of brightly colored panels and leveled text is intended for students in grades 3 through 7"-- Provided by publisher.
  Audience: Ages 7 to 12
  In graphic novel form.
  Includes bibliographical references and index.
  ISBN 978-1-62617-295-1 (hardcover: alk. paper)
  1. Amundsen, Roald, 1872-1928--Juvenile literature. 2. Explorers--Norway--Biography--Juvenile literature. 3. South Pole--Discovery and exploration--Juvenile literature. I. Title.
  G585.A6Y66 2016
  919.89--dc23
                              2015010426

This edition first published in 2016 by Bellwether Media, Inc.

Printed in the United States of America, North Mankato, MN.

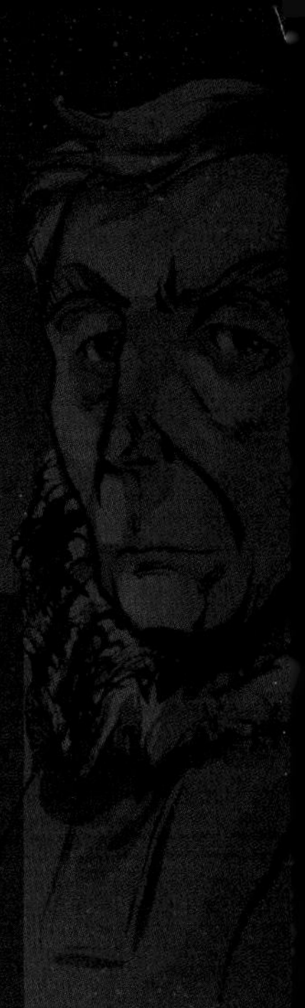

Table of Contents

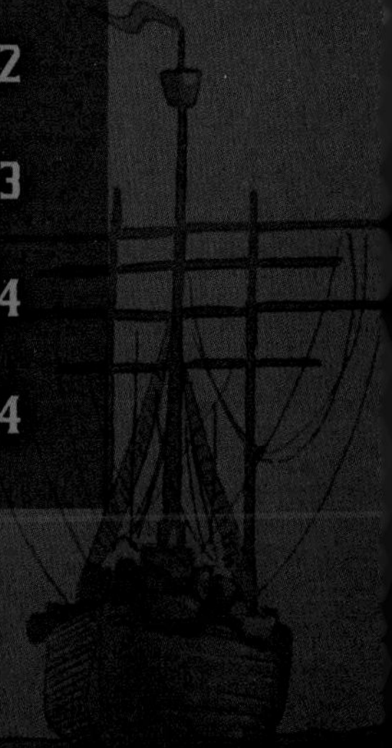

Orange text identifies historical quotes.

THE SECRET PLAN

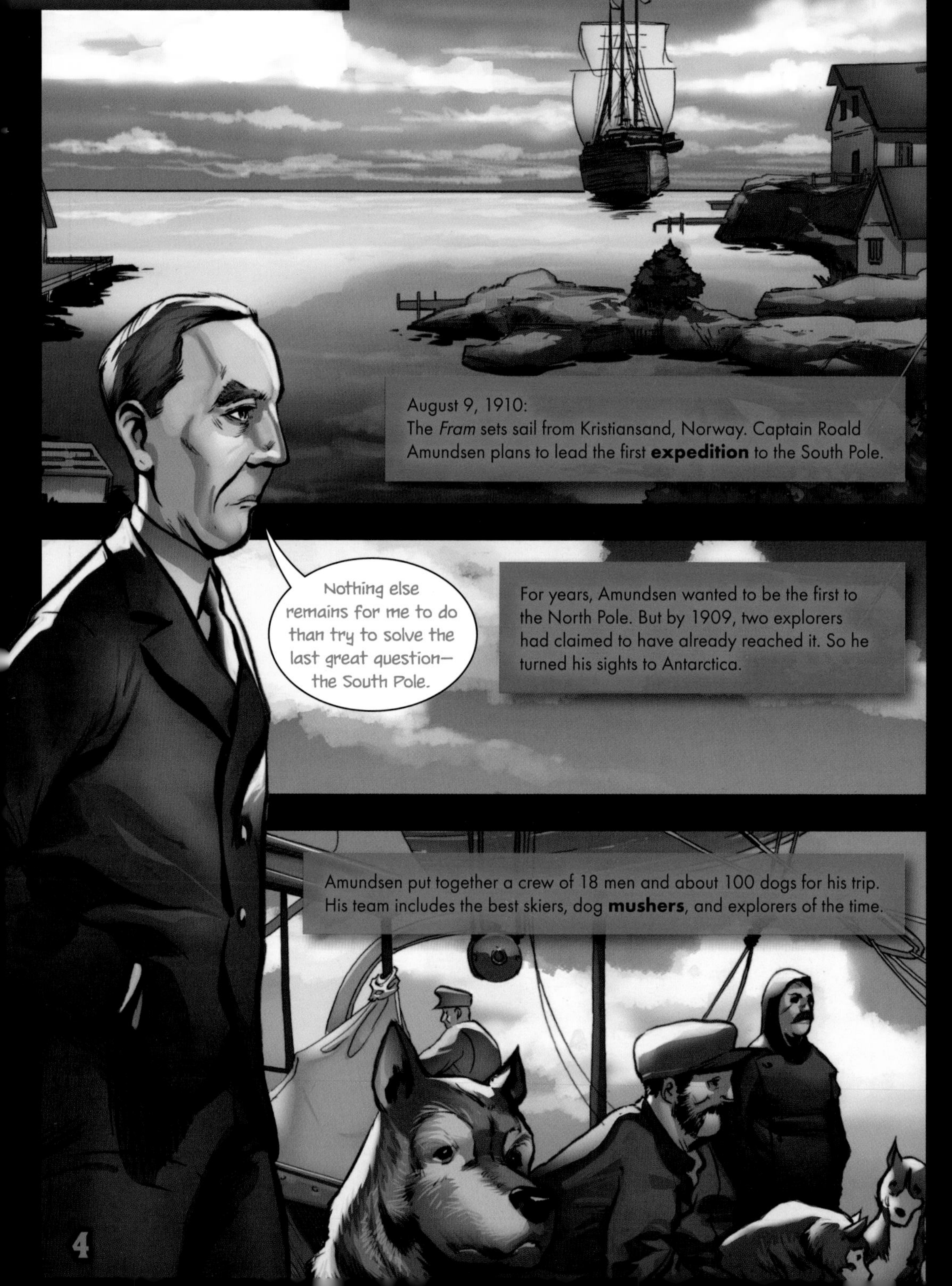
August 9, 1910:
The *Fram* sets sail from Kristiansand, Norway. Captain Roald Amundsen plans to lead the first **expedition** to the South Pole.
Nothing else remains for me to do than try to solve the last great question— the South Pole.
For years, Amundsen wanted to be the first to the North Pole. But by 1909, two explorers had claimed to have already reached it. So he turned his sights to Antarctica.
Amundsen put together a crew of 18 men and about 100 dogs for his trip. His team includes the best skiers, dog **mushers**, and explorers of the time.

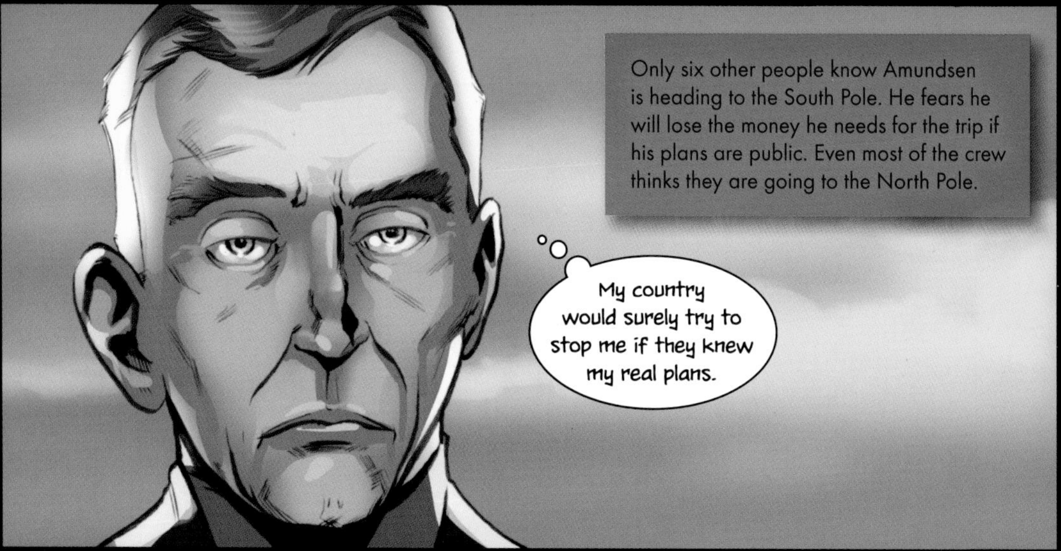
Only six other people know Amundsen is heading to the South Pole. He fears he will lose the money he needs for the trip if his plans are public. Even most of the crew thinks they are going to the North Pole.
My country would surely try to stop me if they knew my real plans.

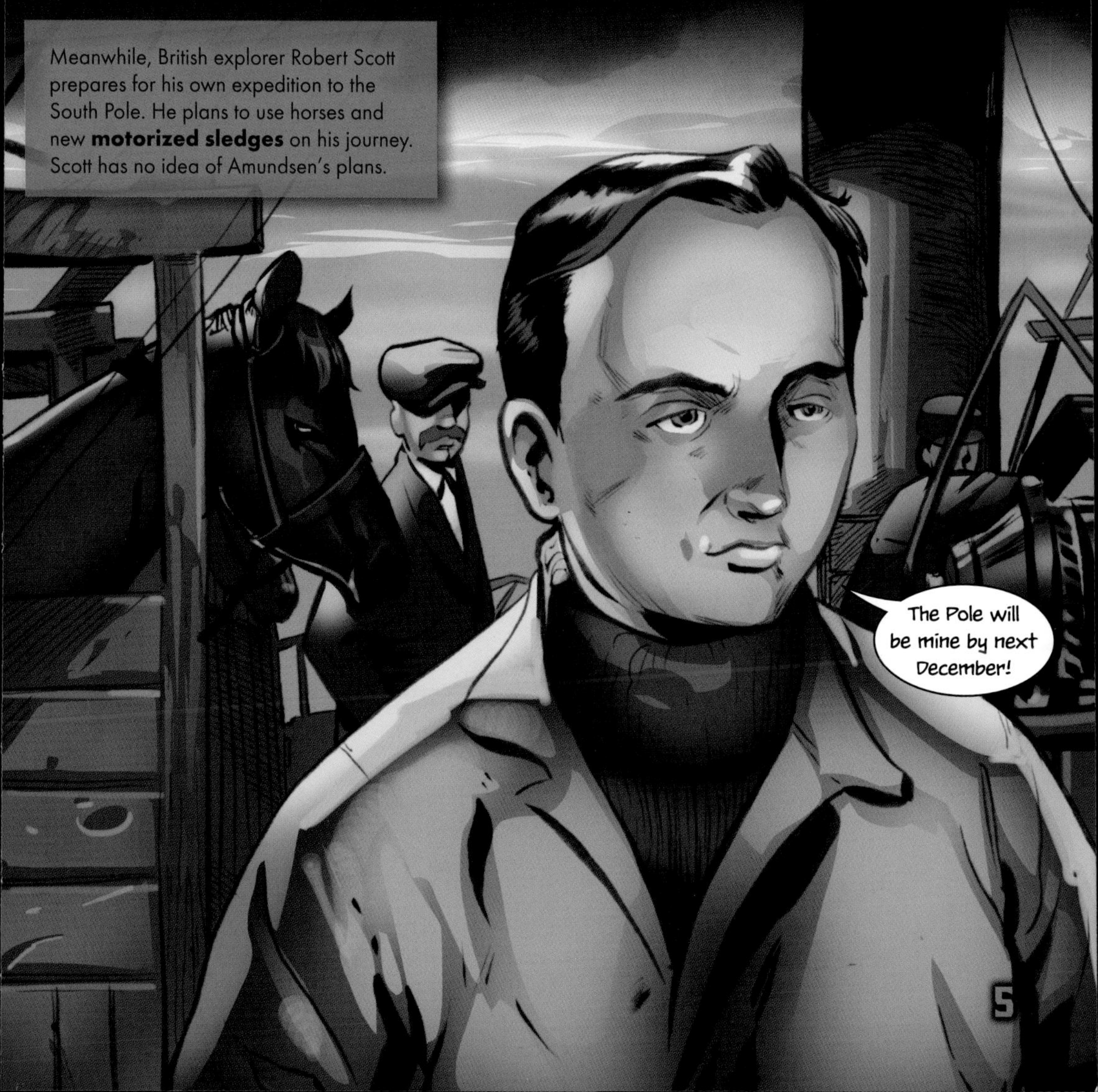
Meanwhile, British explorer Robert Scott prepares for his own expedition to the South Pole. He plans to use horses and new **motorized sledges** on his journey. Scott has no idea of Amundsen's plans.
The Pole will be mine by next December!

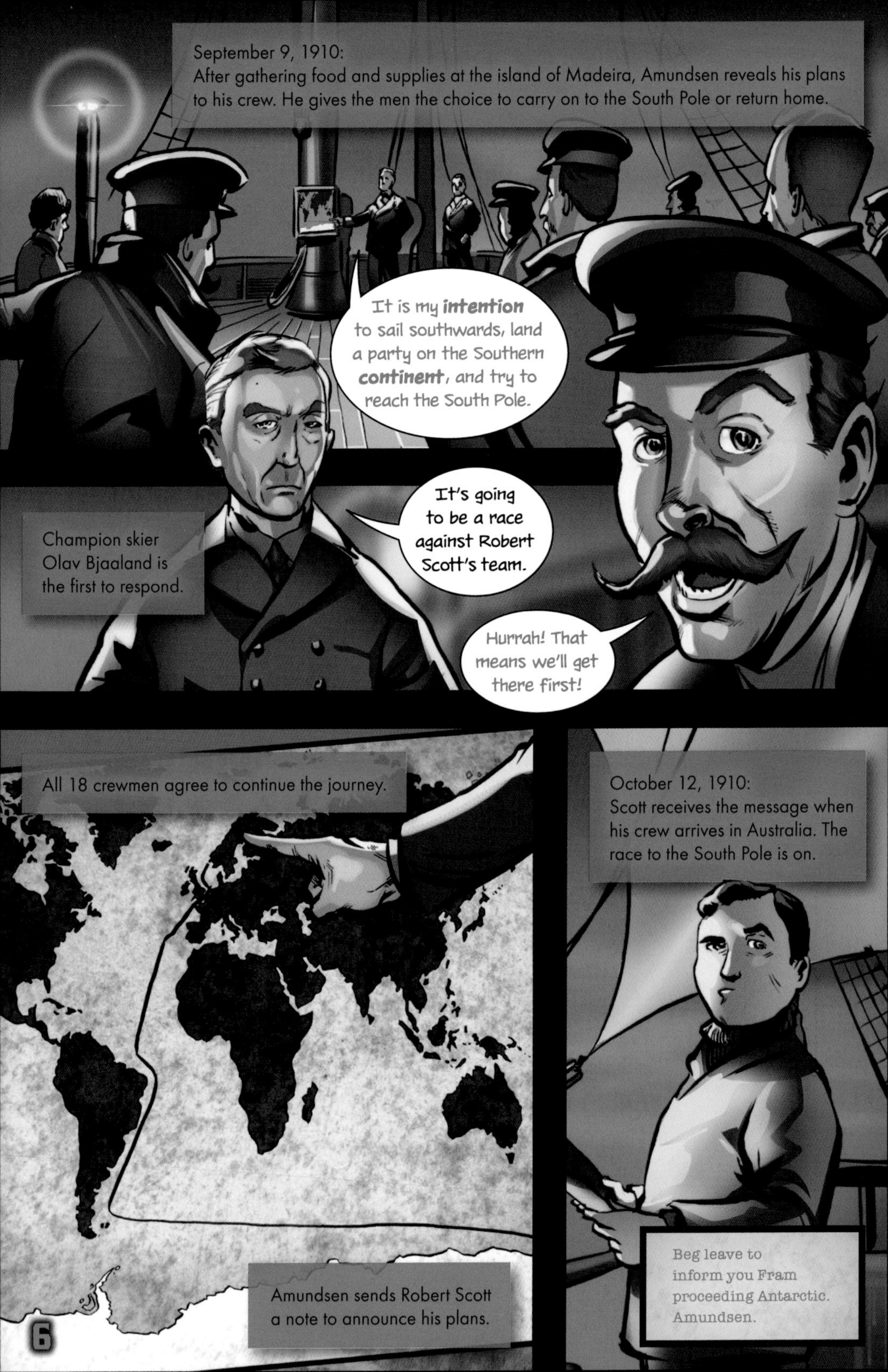
September 9, 1910:
After gathering food and supplies at the island of Madeira, Amundsen reveals his plans to his crew. He gives the men the choice to carry on to the South Pole or return home.
It is my **intention** to sail southwards, land a party on the Southern **continent**, and try to reach the South Pole.
Champion skier Olav Bjaaland is the first to respond.
It's going to be a race against Robert Scott's team.
Hurrah! That means we'll get there first!
All 18 crewmen agree to continue the journey.
Amundsen sends Robert Scott a note to announce his plans.
October 12, 1910:
Scott receives the message when his crew arrives in Australia. The race to the South Pole is on.
Beg leave to inform you Fram proceeding Antarctic. Amundsen.

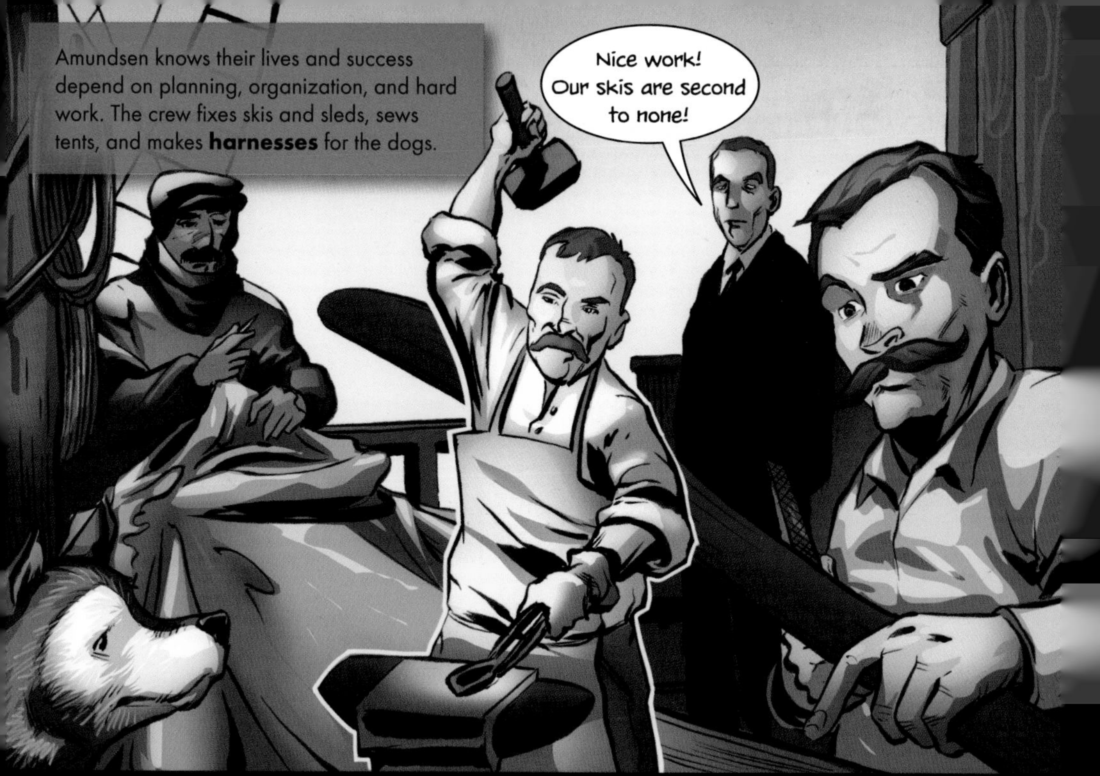
Amundsen knows their lives and success depend on planning, organization, and hard work. The crew fixes skis and sleds, sews tents, and makes **harnesses** for the dogs.
Nice work! Our skis are second to none!

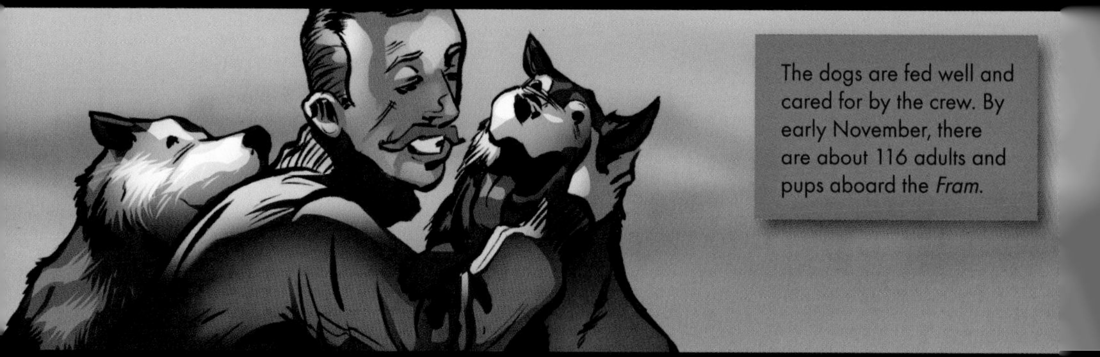
The dogs are fed well and cared for by the crew. By early November, there are about 116 adults and pups aboard the *Fram*.

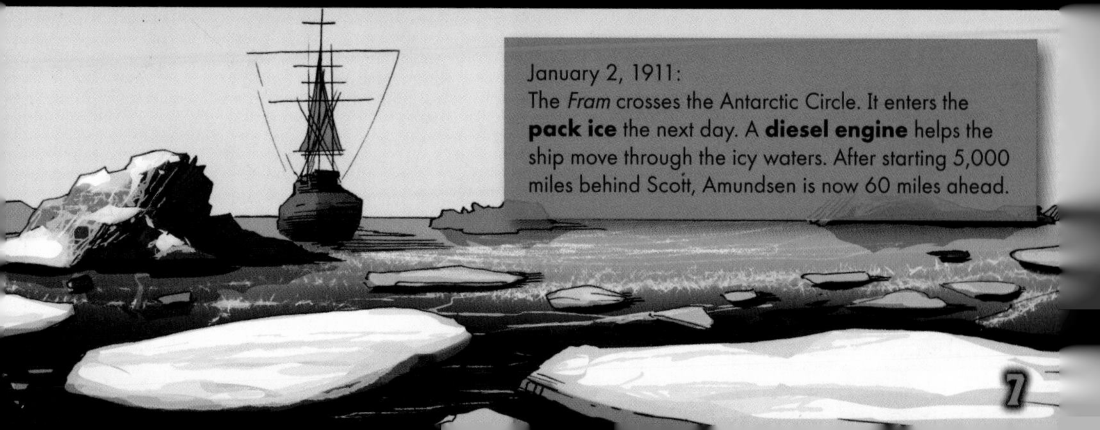
January 2, 1911:
The *Fram* crosses the Antarctic Circle. It enters the **pack ice** the next day. A **diesel engine** helps the ship move through the icy waters. After starting 5,000 miles behind Scott, Amundsen is now 60 miles ahead.

To the Pole!

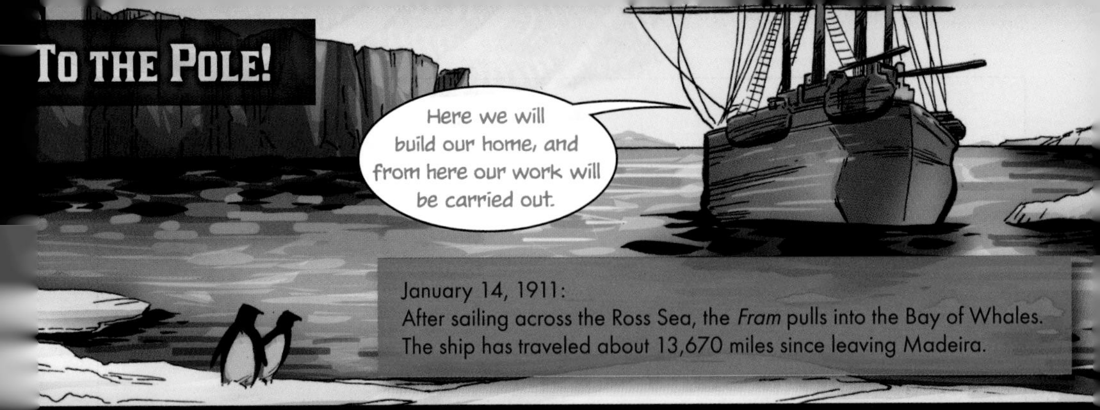
Here we will build our home, and from here our work will be carried out.
January 14, 1911:
After sailing across the Ross Sea, the *Fram* pulls into the Bay of Whales. The ship has traveled about 13,670 miles since leaving Madeira.

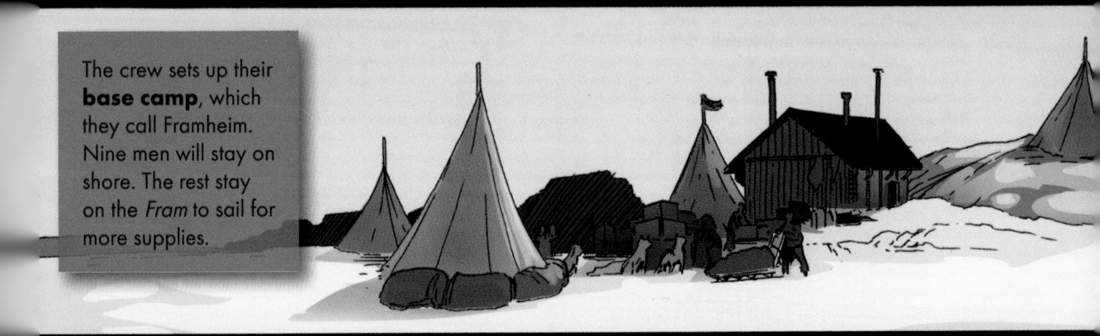
The crew sets up their **base camp**, which they call Framheim. Nine men will stay on shore. The rest stay on the *Fram* to sail for more supplies.

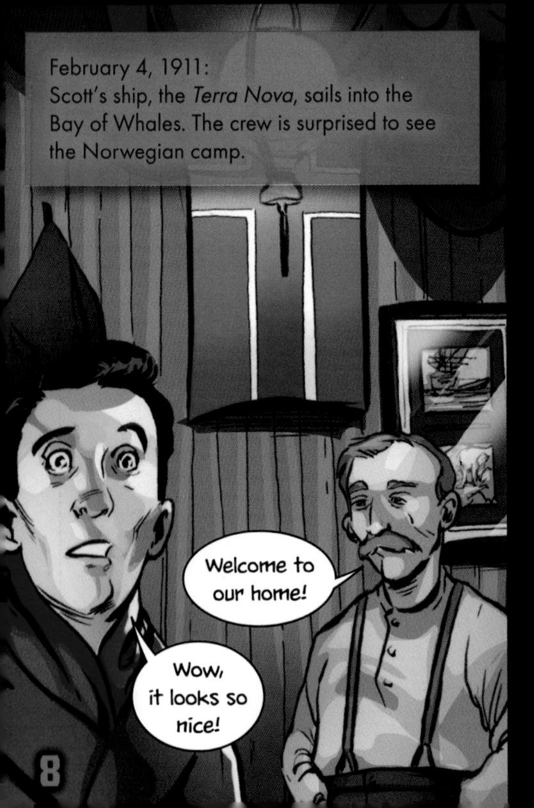
February 4, 1911:
Scott's ship, the *Terra Nova*, sails into the Bay of Whales. The crew is surprised to see the Norwegian camp.
Welcome to our home!
Wow, it looks so nice!

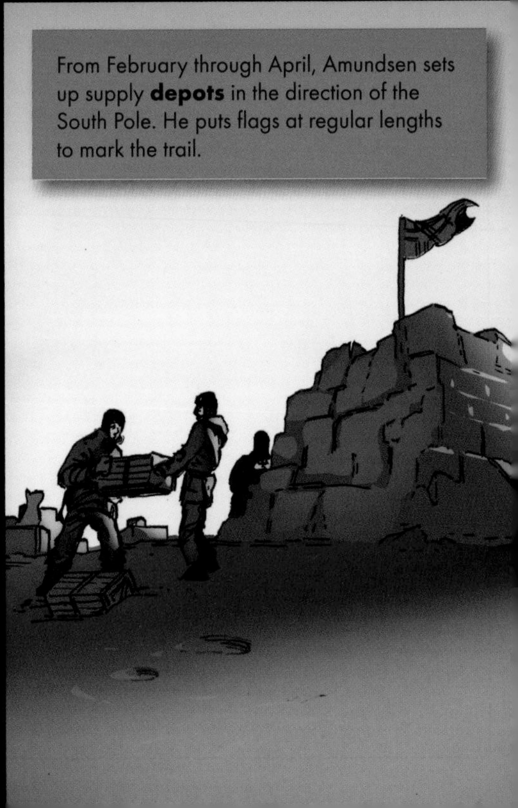
From February through April, Amundsen sets up supply **depots** in the direction of the South Pole. He puts flags at regular lengths to mark the trail.

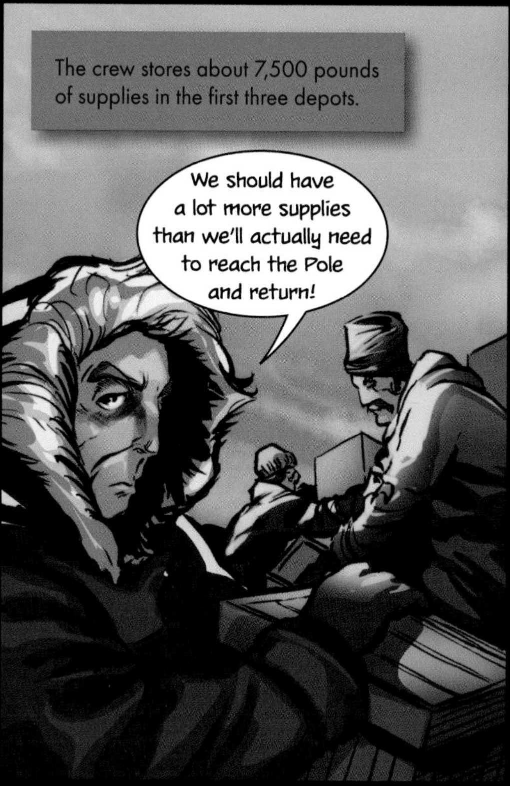
The crew stores about 7,500 pounds of supplies in the first three depots.
We should have a lot more supplies than we'll actually need to reach the Pole and return!

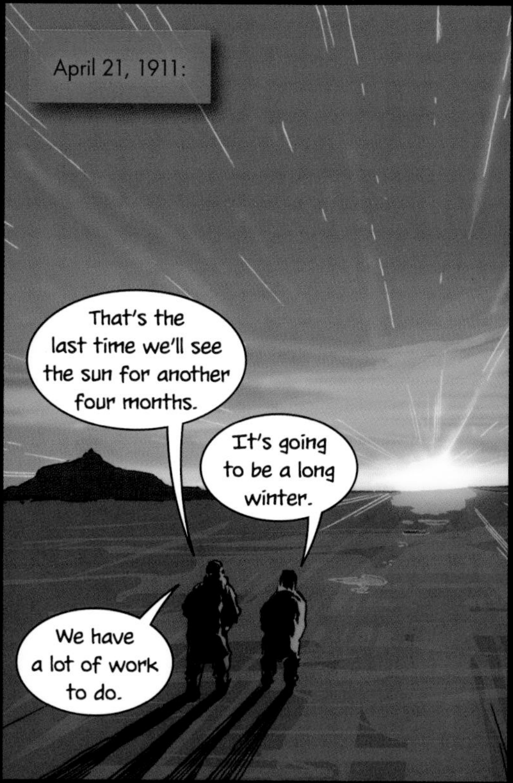
April 21, 1911:
That's the last time we'll see the sun for another four months.
It's going to be a long winter.
We have a lot of work to do.

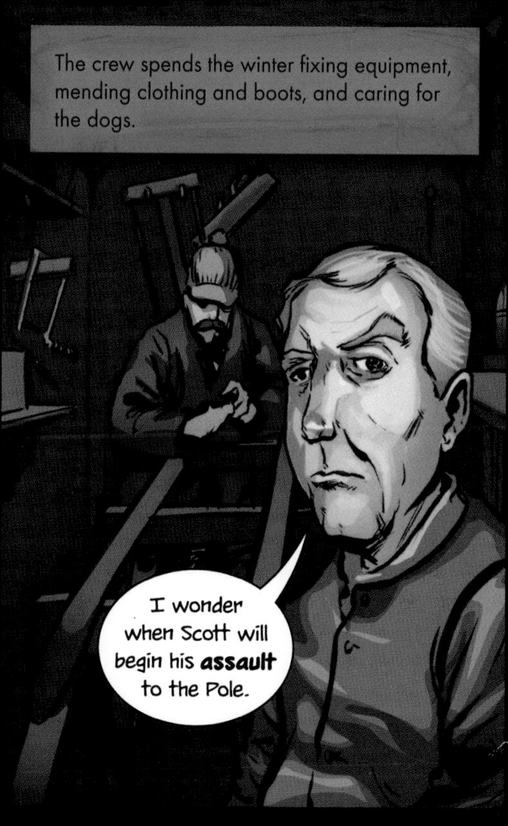
The crew spends the winter fixing equipment, mending clothing and boots, and caring for the dogs.
I wonder when Scott will begin his **assault** to the Pole.

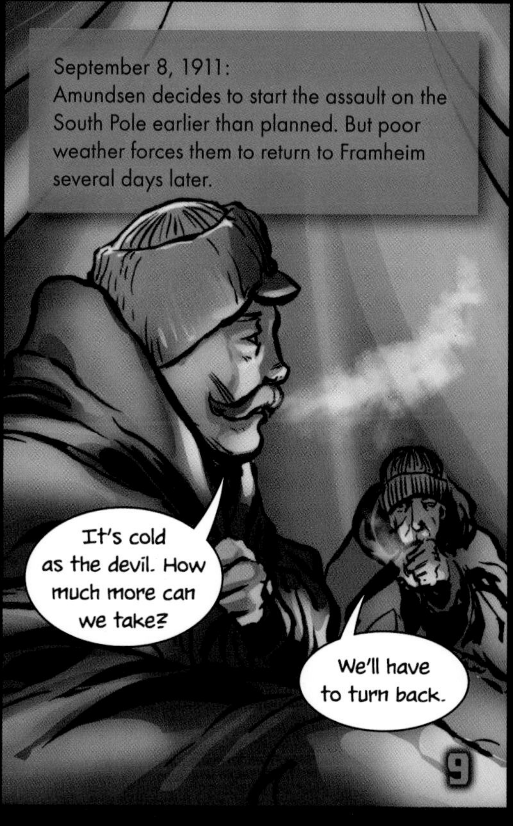
September 8, 1911:
Amundsen decides to start the assault on the South Pole earlier than planned. But poor weather forces them to return to Framheim several days later.
It's cold as the devil. How much more can we take?
We'll have to turn back.

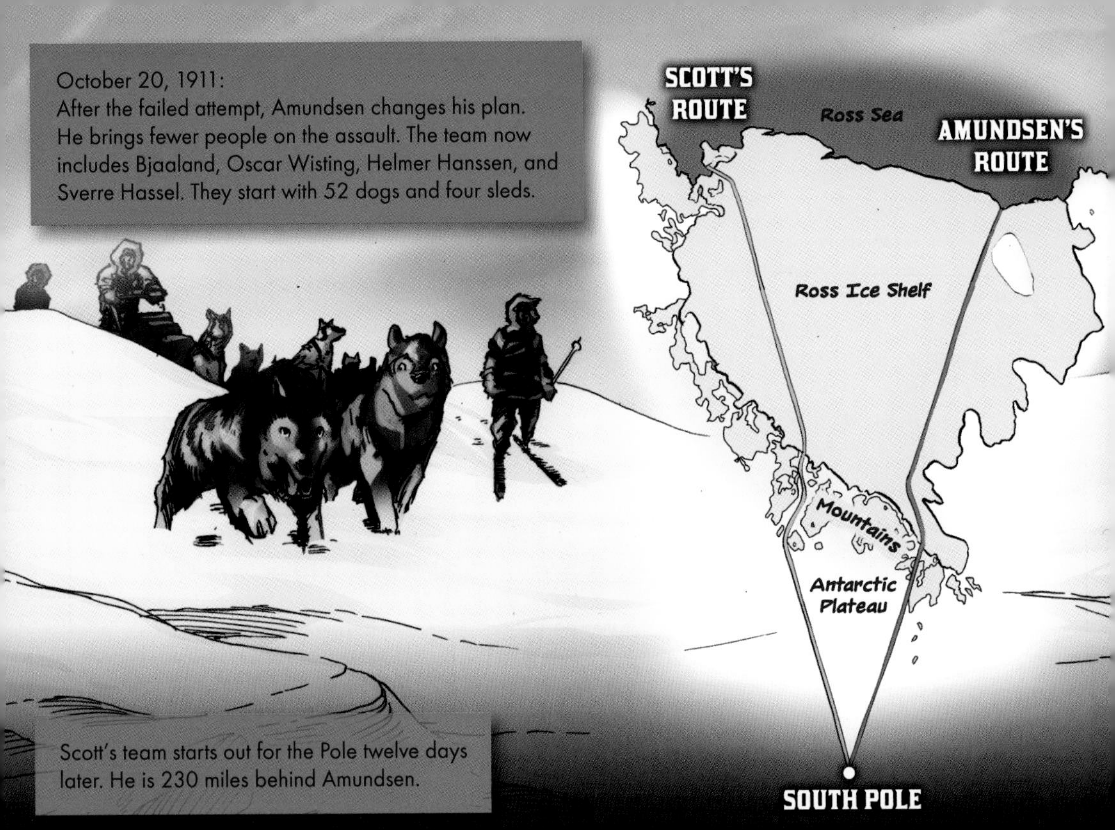
October 20, 1911:
After the failed attempt, Amundsen changes his plan. He brings fewer people on the assault. The team now includes Bjaaland, Oscar Wisting, Helmer Hanssen, and Sverre Hassel. They start with 52 dogs and four sleds.
SCOTT'S ROUTE
Ross Sea
AMUNDSEN'S ROUTE
Ross Ice Shelf
Mountains
Antarctic Plateau
SOUTH POLE
Scott's team starts out for the Pole twelve days later. He is 230 miles behind Amundsen.

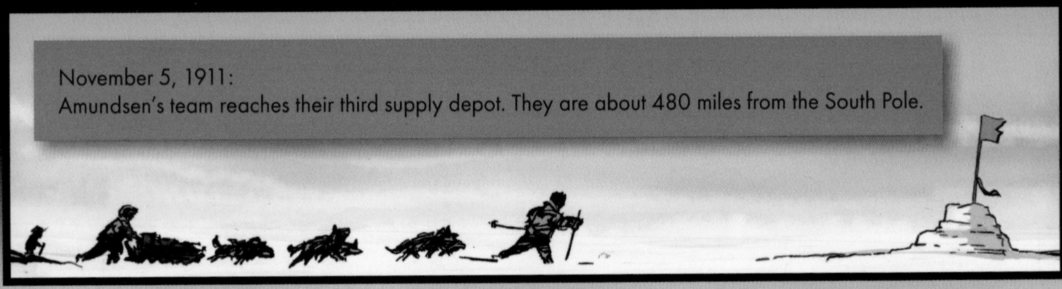
November 5, 1911:
Amundsen's team reaches their third supply depot. They are about 480 miles from the South Pole.

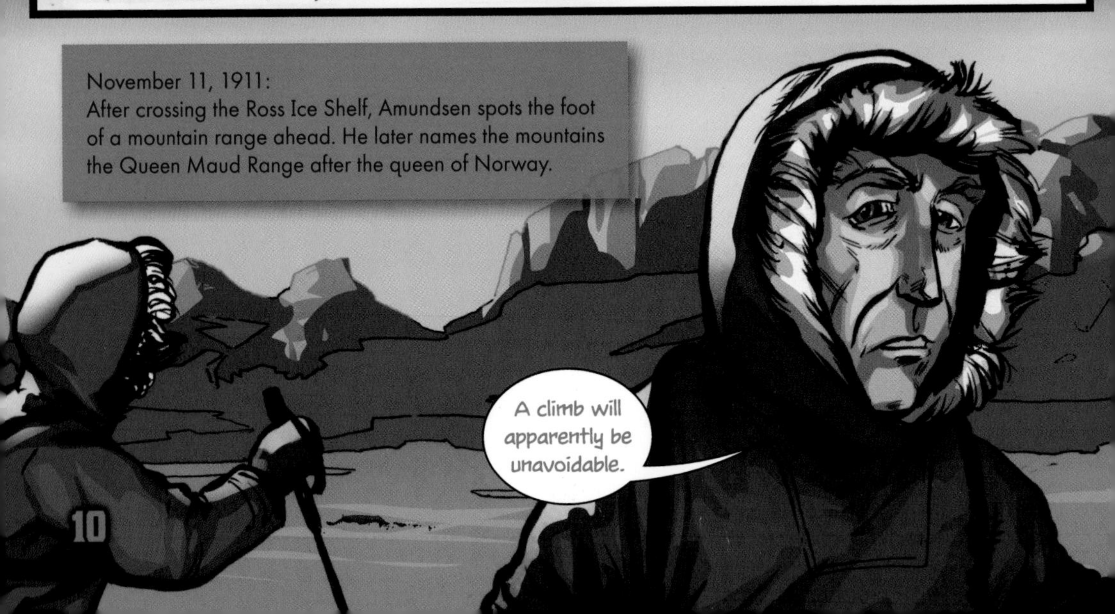
November 11, 1911:
After crossing the Ross Ice Shelf, Amundsen spots the foot of a mountain range ahead. He later names the mountains the Queen Maud Range after the queen of Norway.
A climb will apparently be unavoidable.

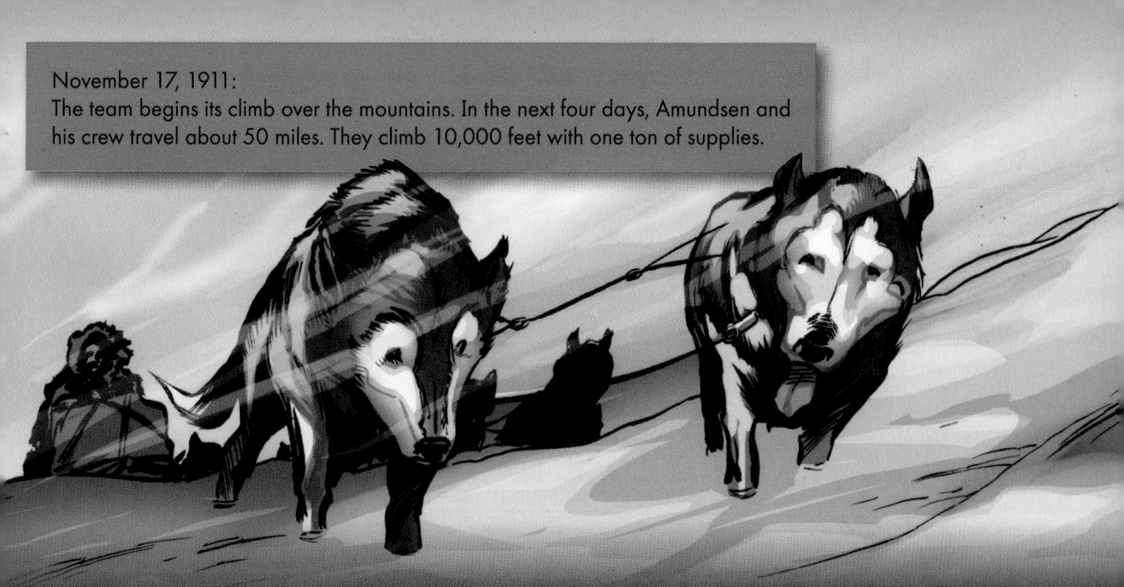
November 17, 1911:
The team begins its climb over the mountains. In the next four days, Amundsen and his crew travel about 50 miles. They climb 10,000 feet with one ton of supplies.

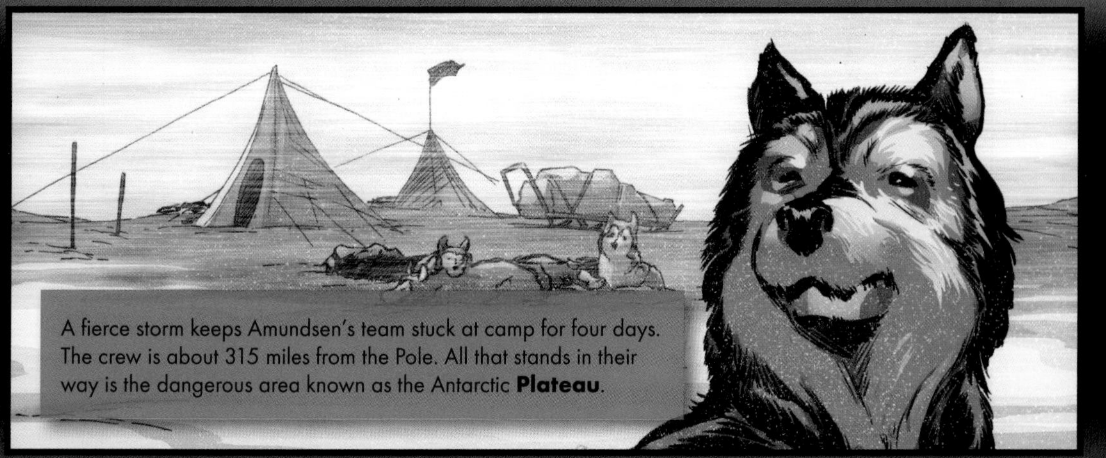
A fierce storm keeps Amundsen's team stuck at camp for four days. The crew is about 315 miles from the Pole. All that stands in their way is the dangerous area known as the Antarctic **Plateau**.

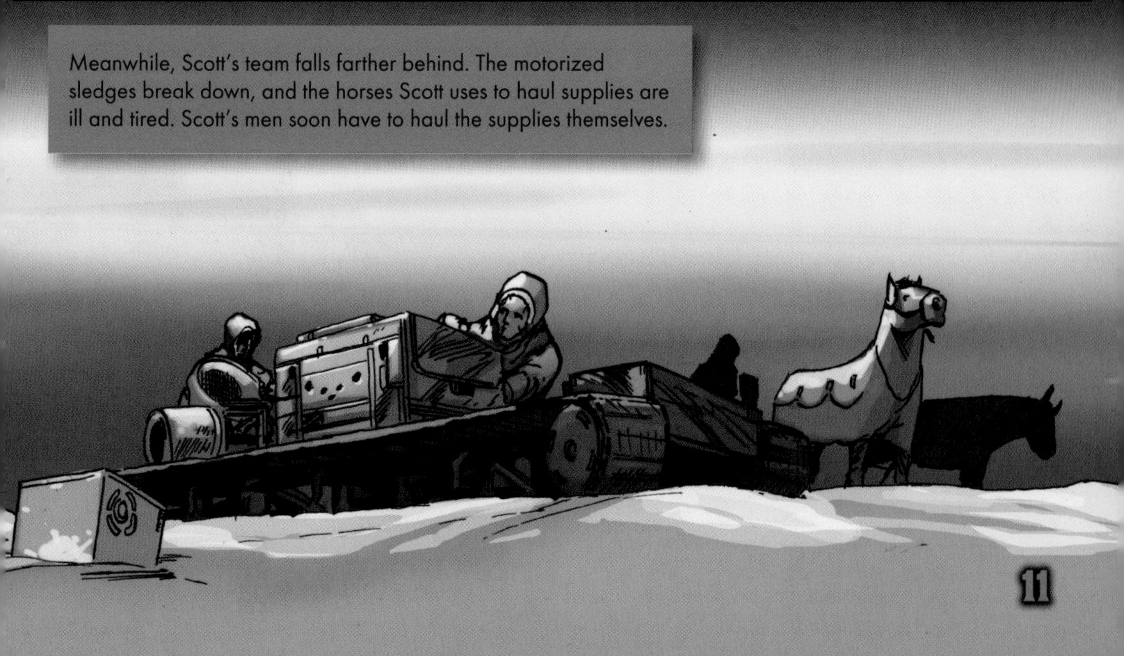
Meanwhile, Scott's team falls farther behind. The motorized sledges break down, and the horses Scott uses to haul supplies are ill and tired. Scott's men soon have to haul the supplies themselves.

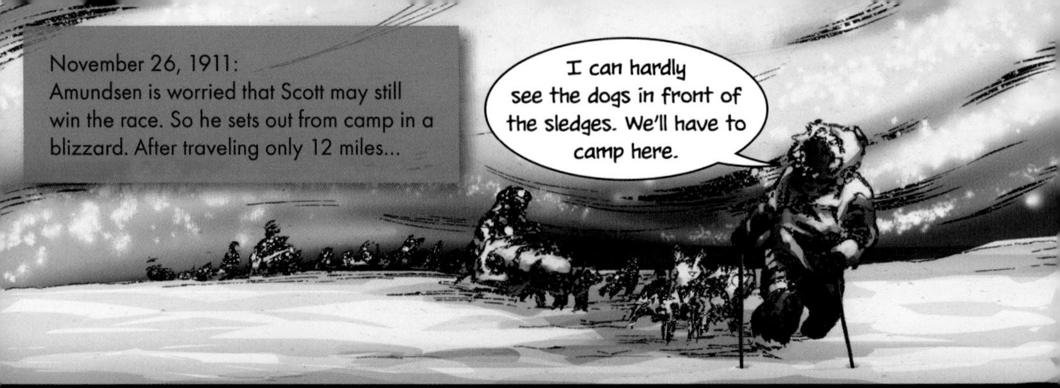
November 26, 1911:
Amundsen is worried that Scott may still win the race. So he sets out from camp in a blizzard. After traveling only 12 miles...
I can hardly see the dogs in front of the sledges. We'll have to camp here.

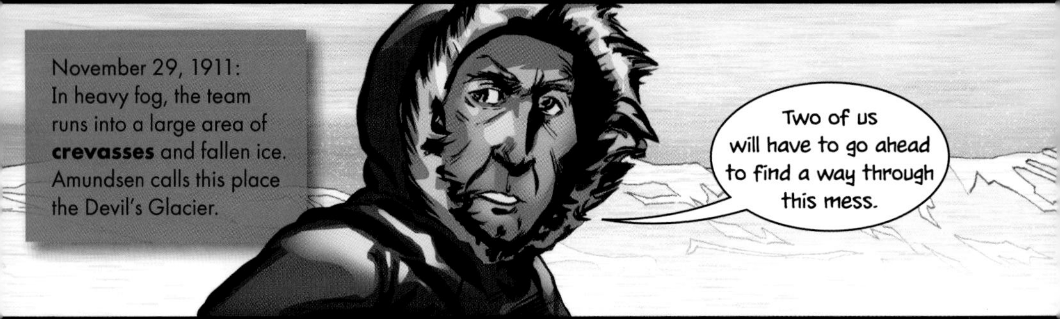
November 29, 1911:
In heavy fog, the team runs into a large area of **crevasses** and fallen ice. Amundsen calls this place the Devil's Glacier.
Two of us will have to go ahead to find a way through this mess.

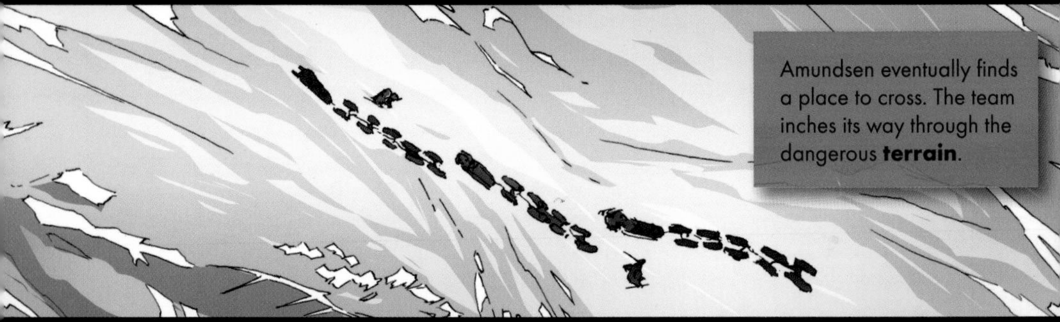
Amundsen eventually finds a place to cross. The team inches its way through the dangerous **terrain**.

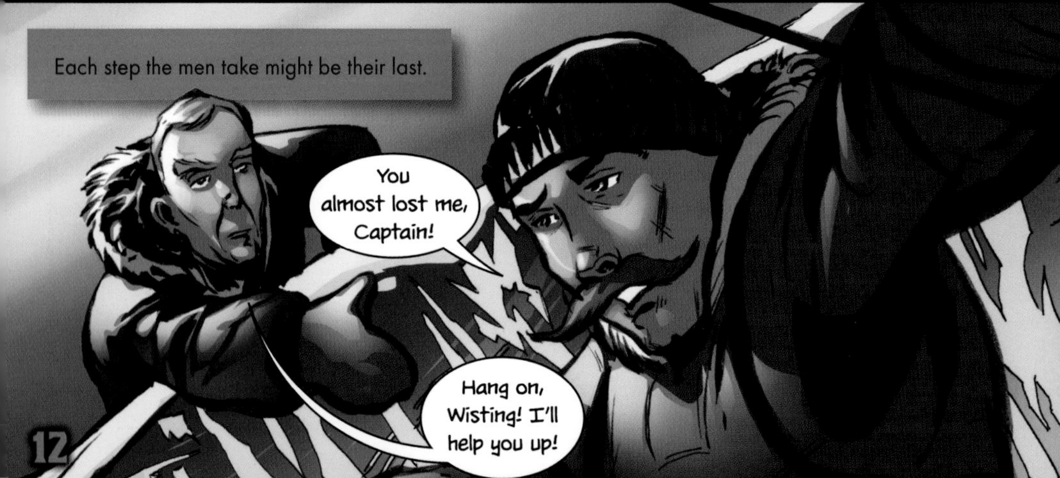
Each step the men take might be their last.
You almost lost me, Captain!
Hang on, Wisting! I'll help you up!

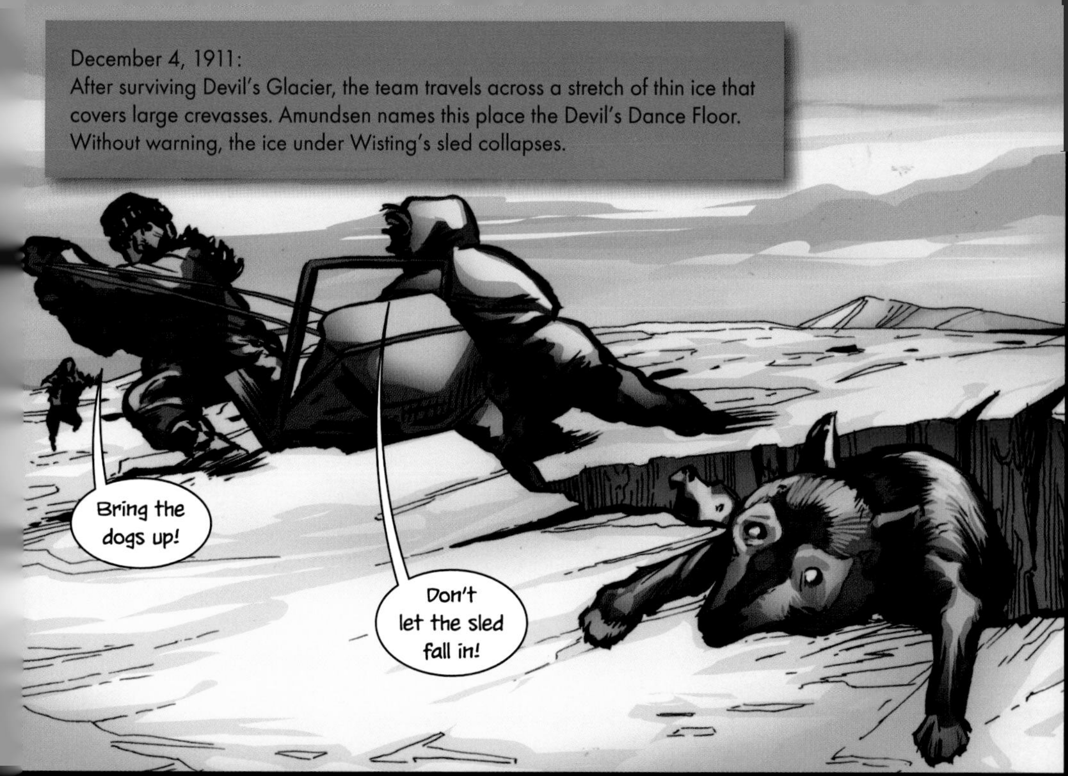
December 4, 1911:
After surviving Devil's Glacier, the team travels across a stretch of thin ice that covers large crevasses. Amundsen names this place the Devil's Dance Floor. Without warning, the ice under Wisting's sled collapses.
Bring the dogs up!
Don't let the sled fall in!

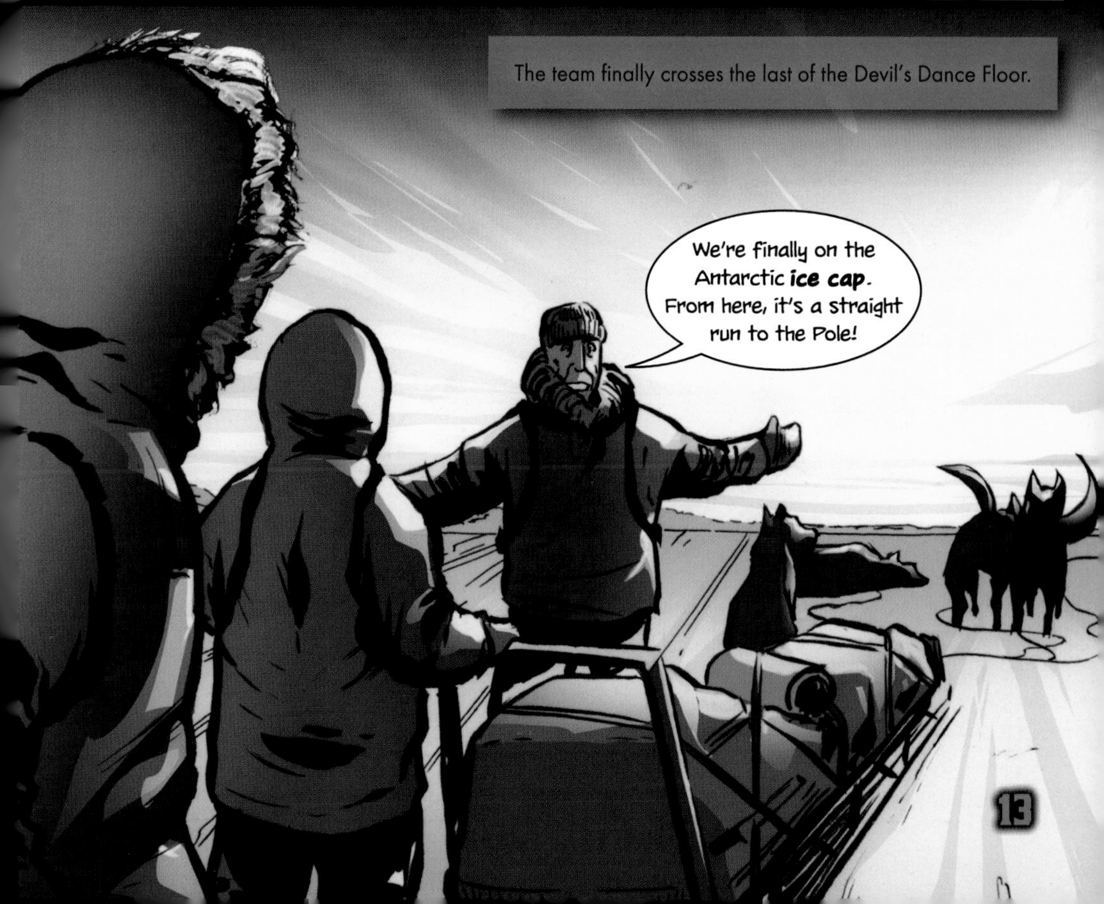
The team finally crosses the last of the Devil's Dance Floor.
We're finally on the Antarctic ice cap. From here, it's a straight run to the Pole!

THE FINAL PUSH

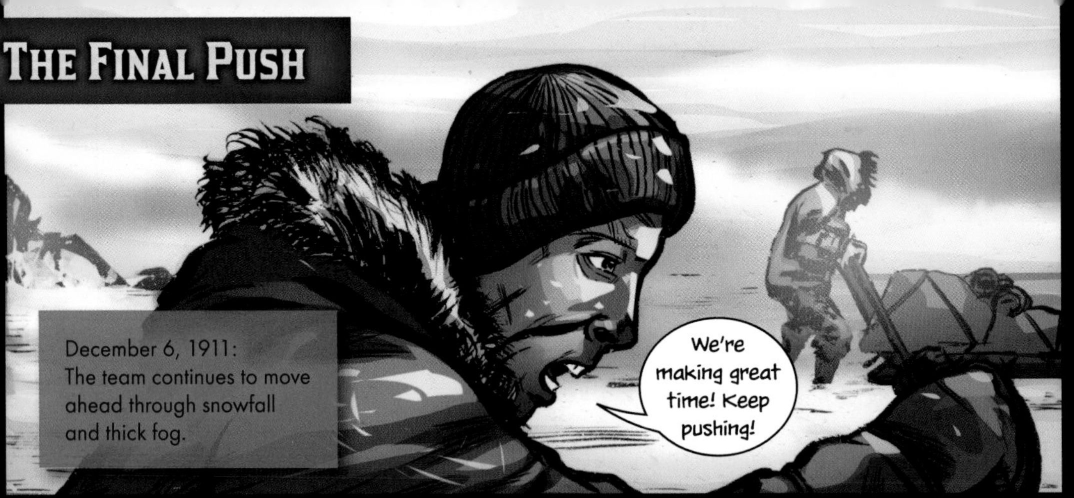
December 6, 1911:
The team continues to move ahead through snowfall and thick fog.
We're making great time! Keep pushing!

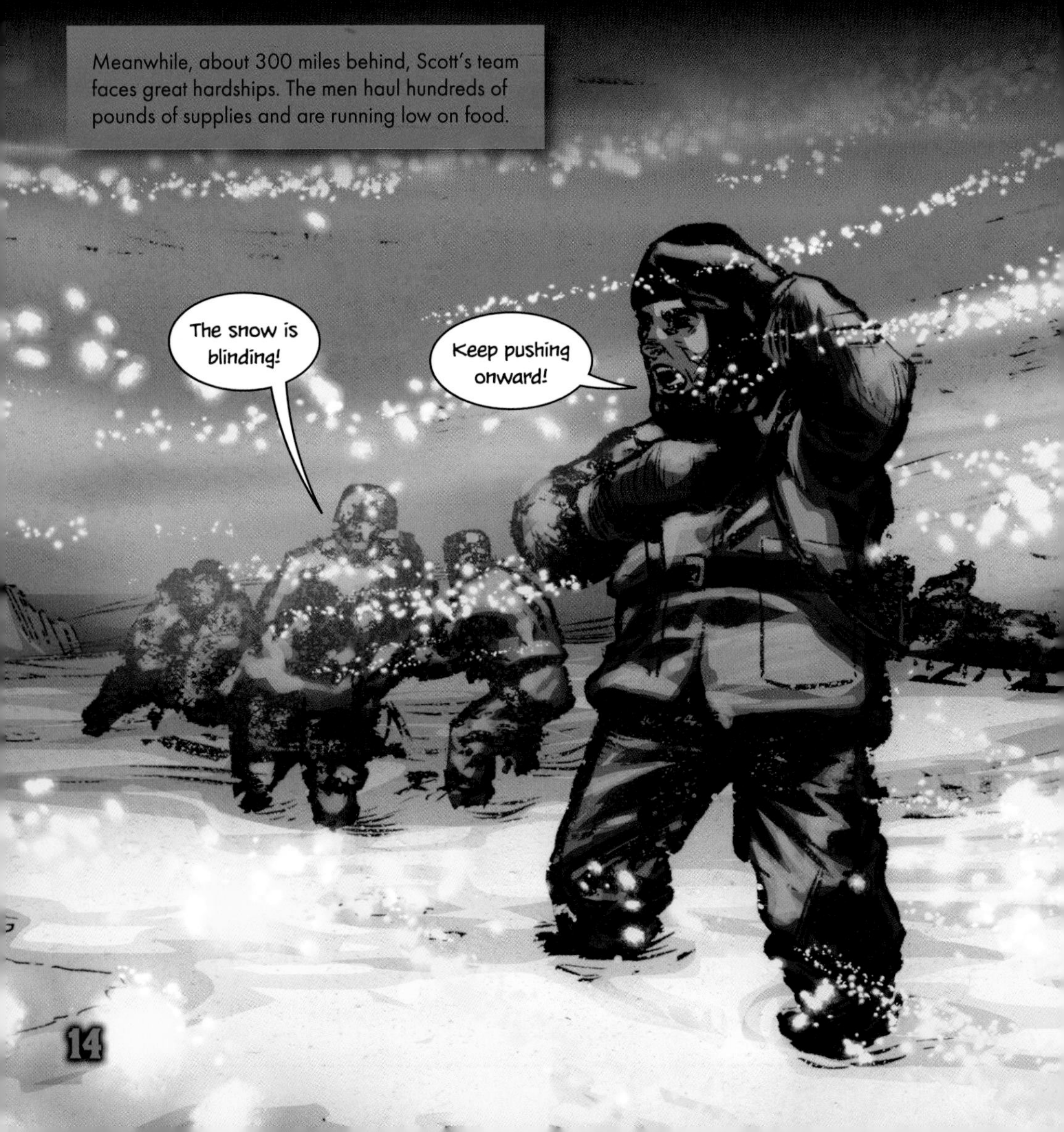
Meanwhile, about 300 miles behind, Scott's team faces great hardships. The men haul hundreds of pounds of supplies and are running low on food.
The snow is blinding!
Keep pushing onward!

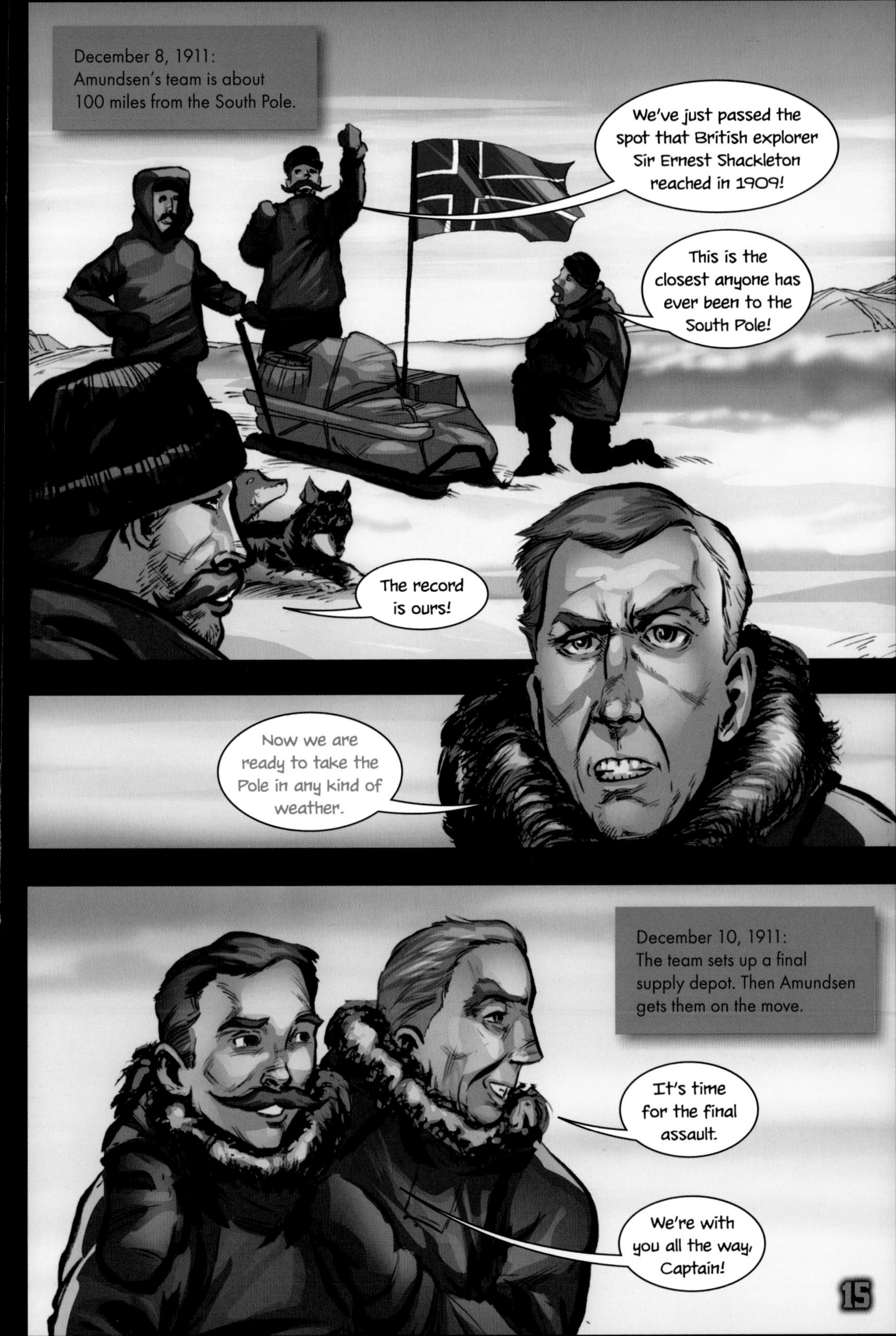
December 8, 1911:
Amundsen's team is about
100 miles from the South Pole.
We've just passed the spot that British explorer Sir Ernest Shackleton reached in 1909!
This is the closest anyone has ever been to the South Pole!
The record is ours!
Now we are ready to take the Pole in any kind of weather.
December 10, 1911:
The team sets up a final supply depot. Then Amundsen gets them on the move.
It's time for the final assault.
We're with you all the way, Captain!

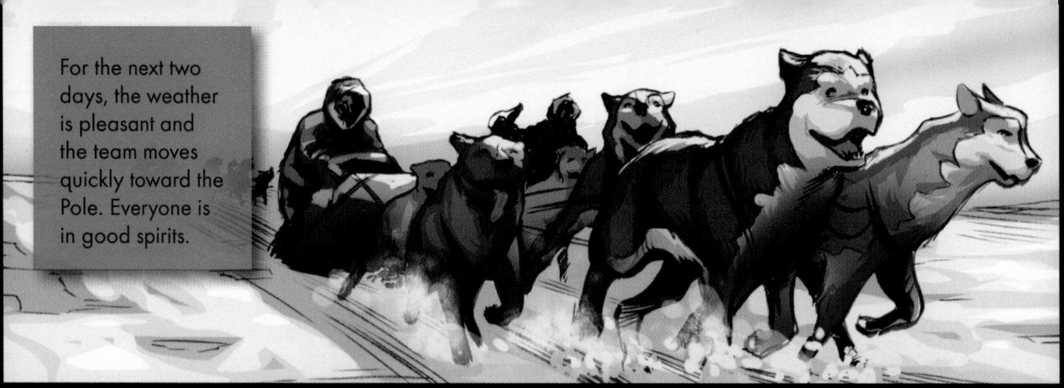
For the next two days, the weather is pleasant and the team moves quickly toward the Pole. Everyone is in good spirits.

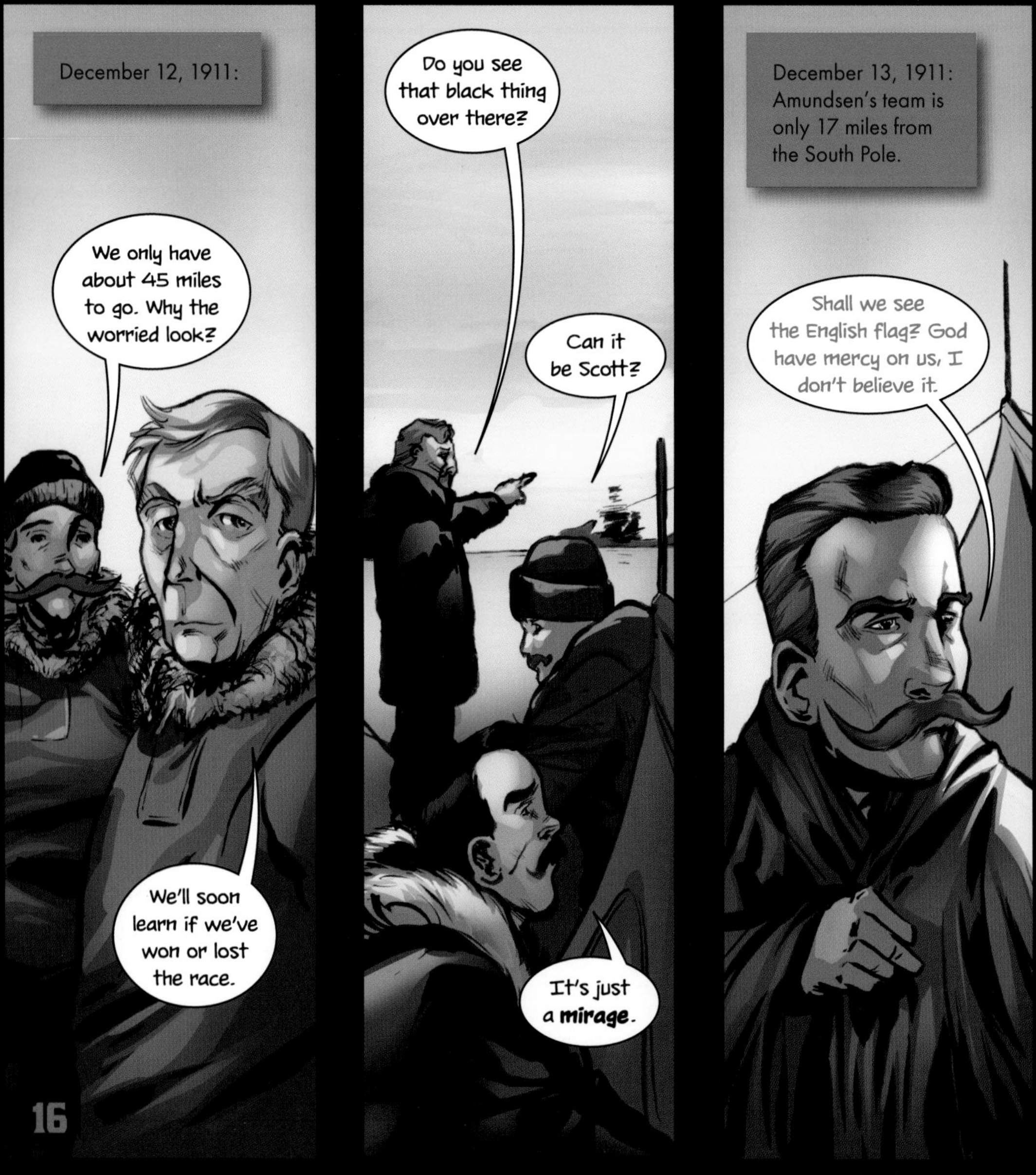
December 12, 1911:
We only have about 45 miles to go. Why the worried look?
We'll soon learn if we've won or lost the race.
Do you see that black thing over there?
Can it be Scott?
It's just a **mirage**.
December 13, 1911: Amundsen's team is only 17 miles from the South Pole.
Shall we see the English flag? God have mercy on us, I don't believe it.

December 14, 1911, 3:00 p.m.
Amundsen's team reaches the South Pole! They have traveled about 850 miles in extreme conditions from Framheim.

We've done it!

Congratulations, Captain!

The men plant the Norwegian flag. They spend the next three days making sure they are at the exact location of the Pole.

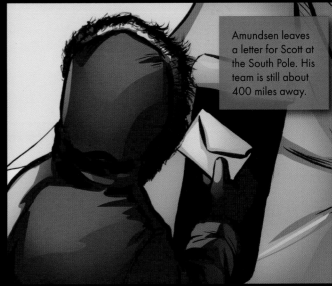

Amundsen leaves a letter for Scott at the South Pole. His team is still about 400 miles away.

December 18, 1911:
The time comes for Amundsen's team to travel back to Framheim.

And so, farewell, dear Pole. I don't think we'll meet again.

HOMEWARD BOUND

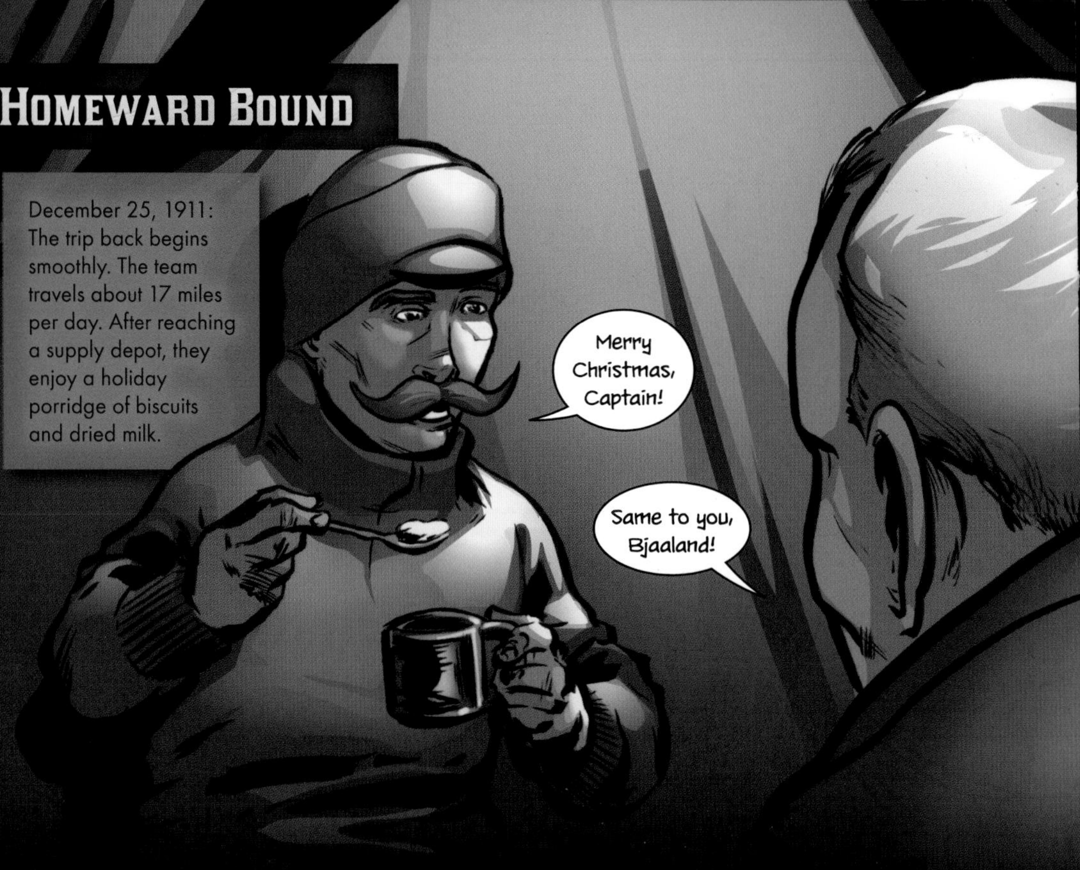
December 25, 1911: The trip back begins smoothly. The team travels about 17 miles per day. After reaching a supply depot, they enjoy a holiday porridge of biscuits and dried milk.
Merry Christmas, Captain!
Same to you, Bjaaland!

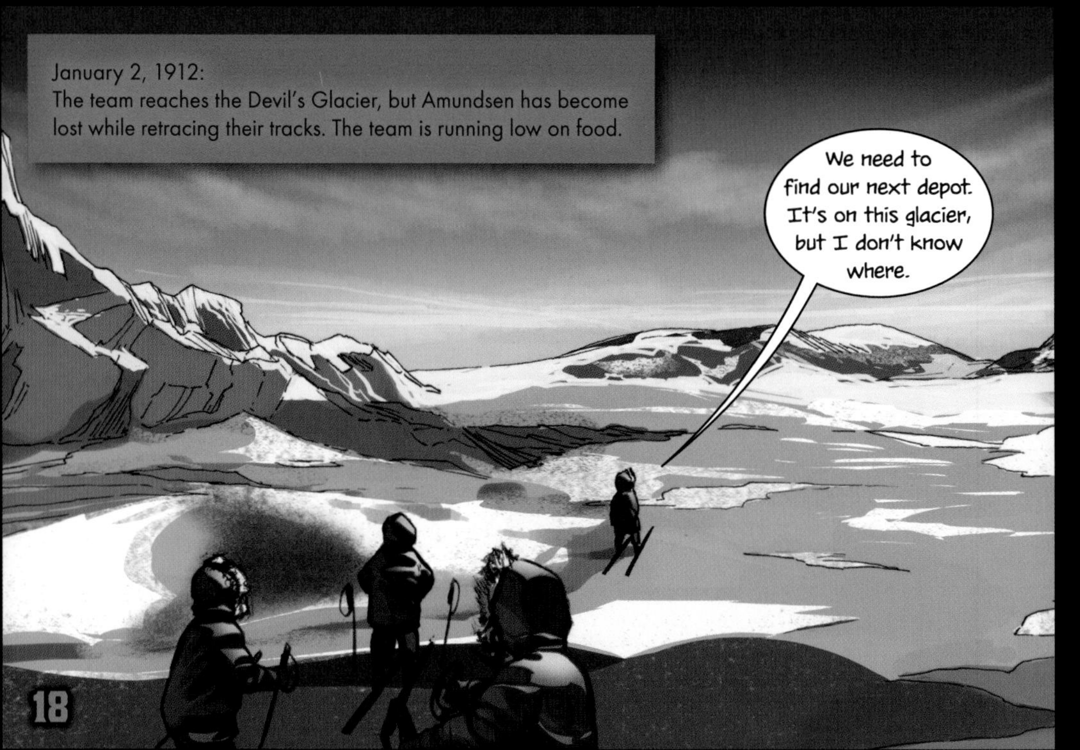
January 2, 1912:
The team reaches the Devil's Glacier, but Amundsen has become lost while retracing their tracks. The team is running low on food.
We need to find our next depot. It's on this glacier, but I don't know where.

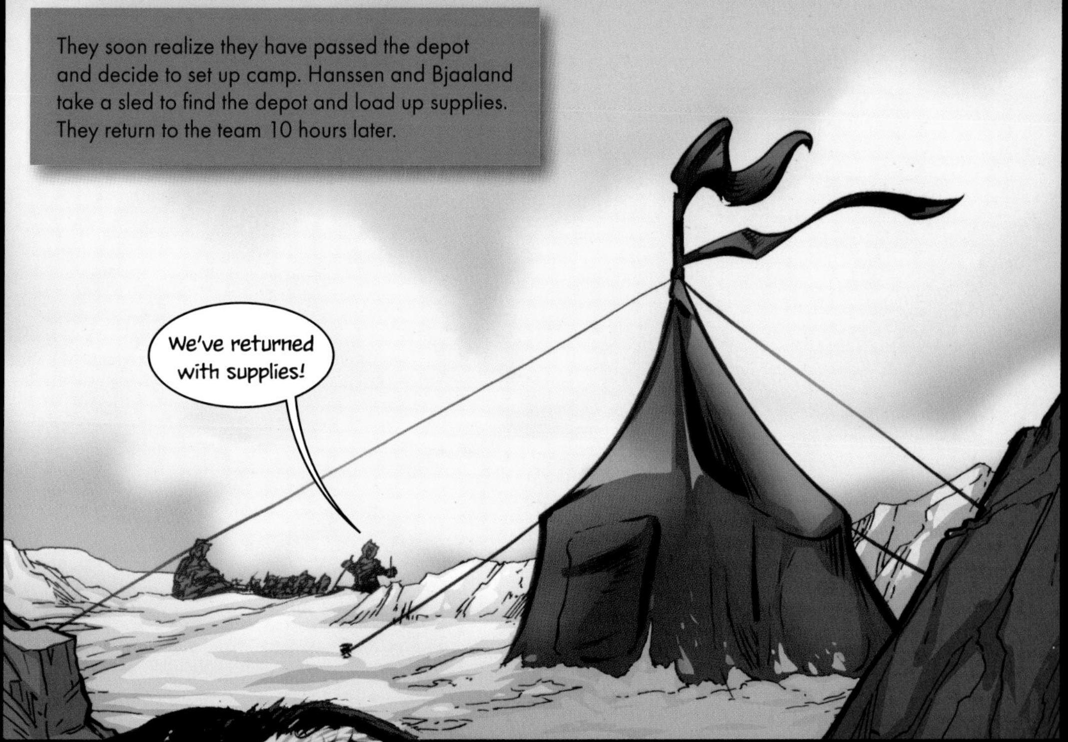
They soon realize they have passed the depot and decide to set up camp. Hanssen and Bjaaland take a sled to find the depot and load up supplies. They return to the team 10 hours later.
We've returned with supplies!

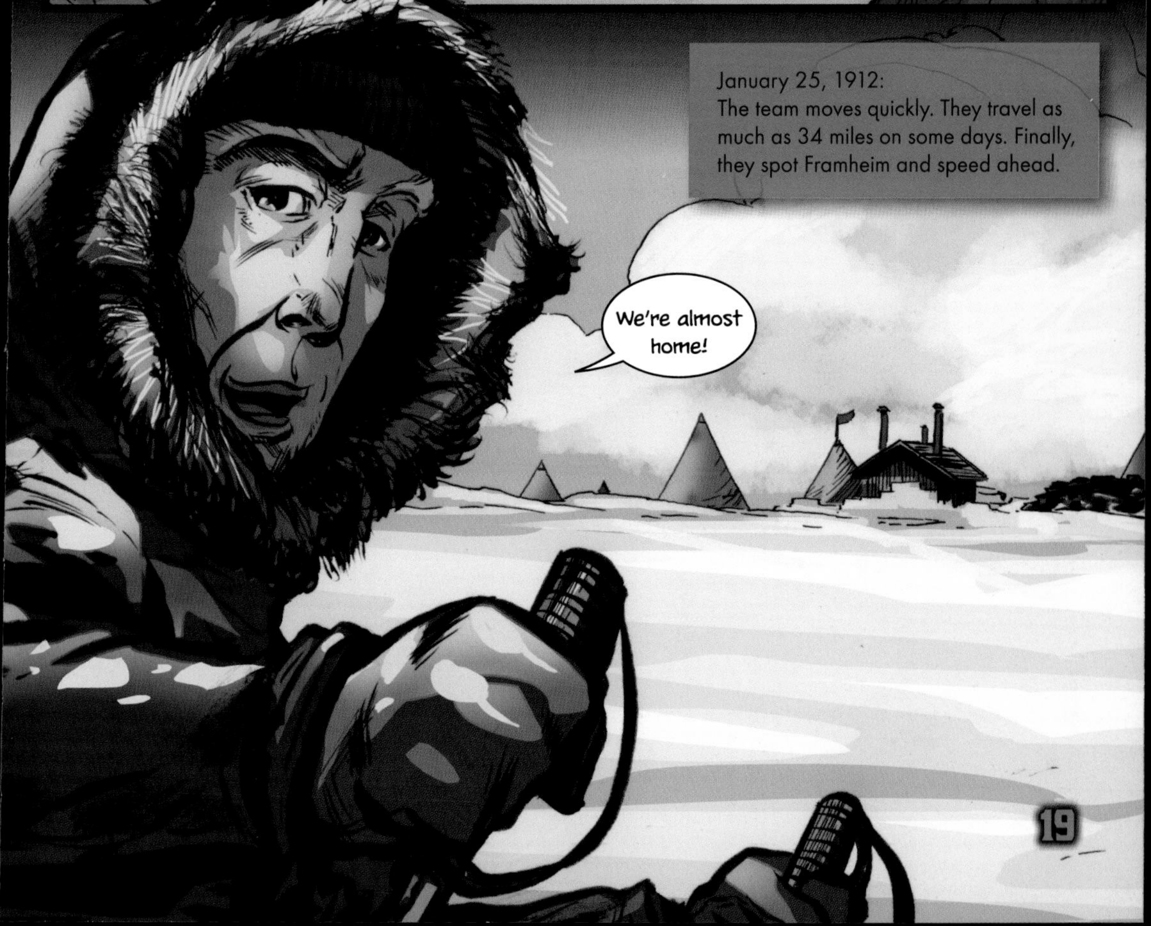
January 25, 1912:
The team moves quickly. They travel as much as 34 miles on some days. Finally, they spot Framheim and speed ahead.
We're almost home!

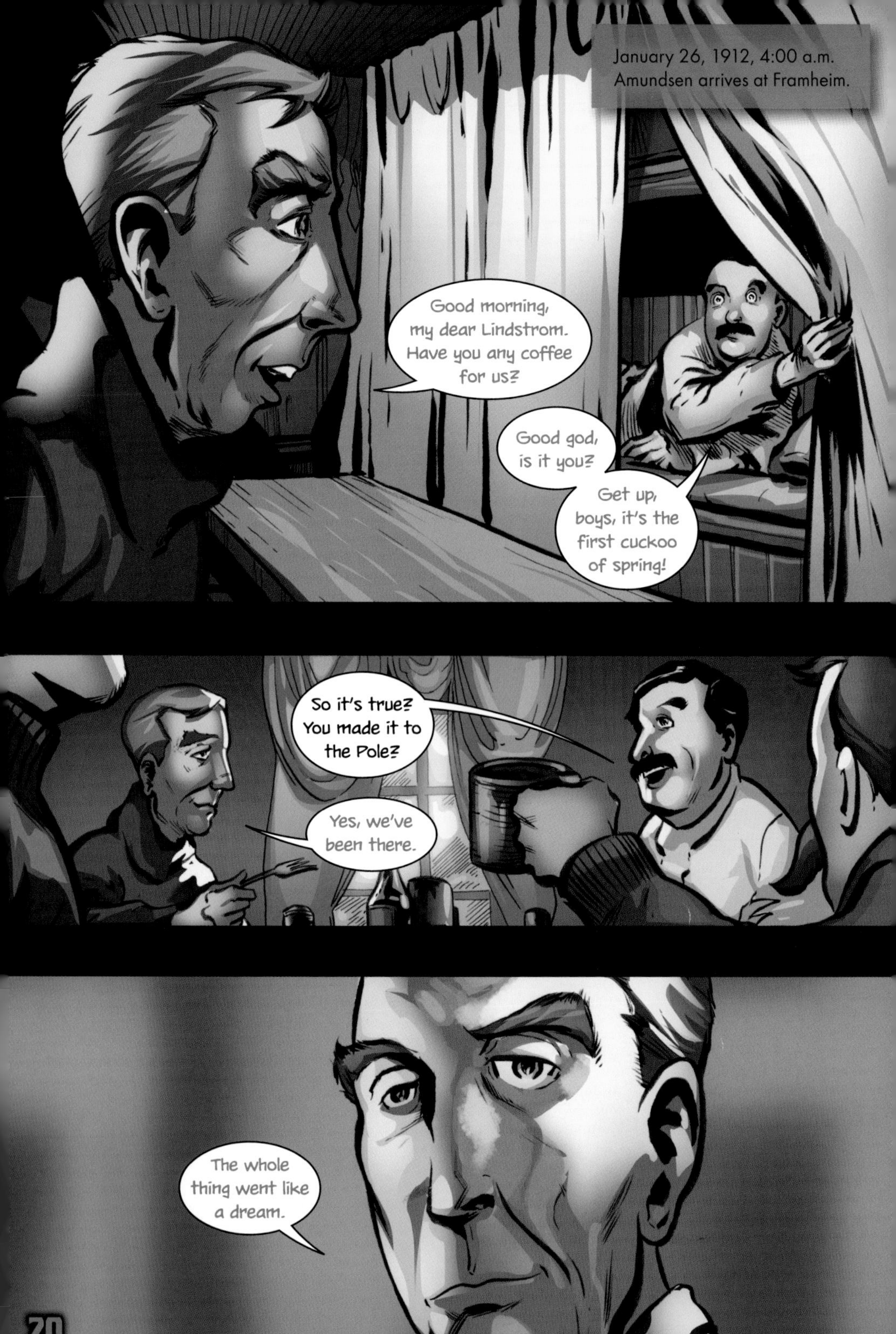
January 26, 1912, 4:00 a.m. Amundsen arrives at Framheim.
Good morning, my dear Lindstrom. Have you any coffee for us?
Good god, is it you?
Get up, boys, it's the first cuckoo of spring!
So it's true? You made it to the Pole?
Yes, we've been there.
The whole thing went like a dream.

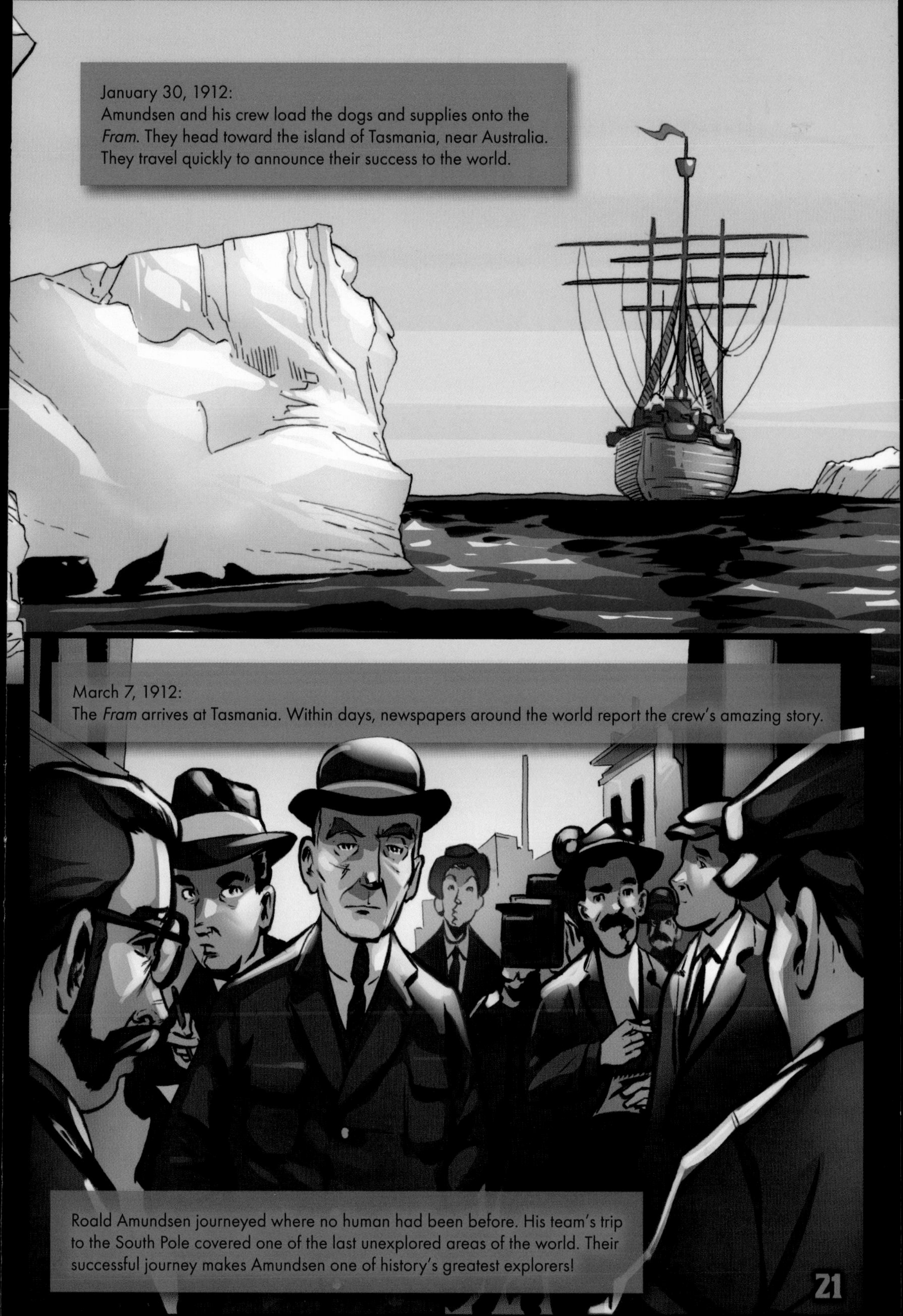
January 30, 1912:
Amundsen and his crew load the dogs and supplies onto the *Fram*. They head toward the island of Tasmania, near Australia. They travel quickly to announce their success to the world.
March 7, 1912:
The *Fram* arrives at Tasmania. Within days, newspapers around the world report the crew's amazing story.
Roald Amundsen journeyed where no human had been before. His team's trip to the South Pole covered one of the last unexplored areas of the world. Their successful journey makes Amundsen one of history's greatest explorers!

More About Roald Amundsen and Polar Exploration

- Roald Amundsen attended medical school, but he dropped out at age 21 to become an explorer.
- *Framheim* means "home of the *Fram*" in Norwegian.
- The *Fram* was used for two expeditions in the Arctic before Amundsen sailed it to Antarctica.
- Frederick Cook and Robert Peary were the first two explorers who claimed to have reached the North Pole.
- Robert Scott finally reached the South Pole on January 17, 1912. Tragically, he never made it back to announce their accomplishment. His team died of hunger and exhaustion on their trip back from the Pole.

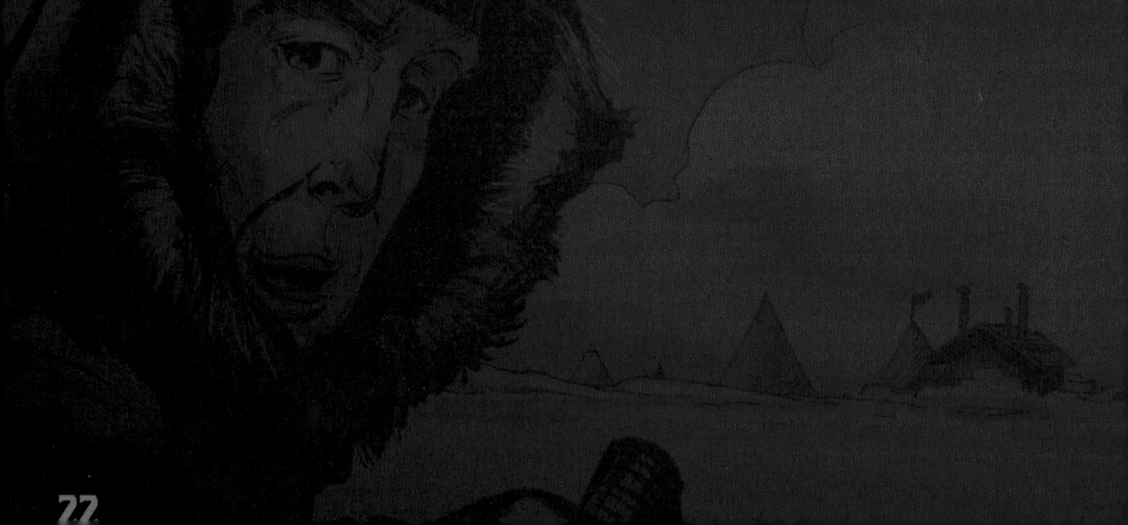

GLOSSARY

assault—an attempt to reach a faraway place

base camp—the first camp from which an expedition sets out

continent—one of the seven large pieces of land in the world

crevasses—deep cracks in a glacier

depots—places where supplies are stored

diesel engine—a type of engine used in large vehicles

expedition—a long trip made for a specific purpose

harnesses—straps connecting dogs to each other to pull a sled

ice cap—a large, thick sheet of ice covering the South Pole

intention—a plan to achieve something

mirage—something seen but actually not there

motorized sledges—heavy sleds powered by motors

mushers—people who drive dogsleds

pack ice—a large sheet of floating ice made up of smaller pieces that have frozen together

plateau—a large, flat area of land higher than the ground around it

terrain—a particular type of land

To Learn More

AT THE LIBRARY

Llanas, Sheila Griffin. *Who Reached the South Pole First?* Mankato, Minn.: Capstone Press, 2011.

Pipe, Jim. *The Race to the South Pole.* Columbus, Ohio: School Specialty Publishing, 2006.

Yomtov, Nel. *Trapped in Antarctica!: Nickolas Flux and the Shackleton Expedition.* North Mankato, Minn.: Capstone Press, 2015.

ON THE WEB

Learning more about Roald Amundsen is as easy as 1, 2, 3.

1. Go to www.factsurfer.com.
2. Enter "Roald Amundsen" into the search box.
3. Click the "Surf" button and you will see a list of related web sites.

With factsurfer.com, finding more information is just a click away.

Index